DISNEY'S THE BLACK CAULDRON

MOUSE WORKS

In the distant land of Prydain lived an old farmer named Dallben. He kept ducks and geese, cats and dogs, and a small blue-eyed pig called Hen Wen. His young apprentice, Taran, helped him take care of the anim

Life on the farm was peaceful and happy – until the day when Dallben hurried home with some very bad news. "Whatever shall we do?" he muttered. "I knew there was something wrong. I felt it in my bones."

Dallben was talking to himself, but his red tomcat jumped onto the table to listen. "As I passed through the woods," the farmer told him, "I heard that the evil Horned King is about to invade Prydain!" Dallben peered anxiously at his old parchment map. "The Fair Folk have gone into hiding," he said. "They know what's coming."

But young Taran wasn't afraid when he heard the news. "At last, I shall be a warrior!" he shouted. Snatching up a stick, he waved it like a sword. "On guard, scoundrels! Your time has come!" he cried.

The ducks and geese squawked angrily, but Taran paid no attention—until Dallben broke into his daydream. "Taran, what are you doing? Taran?"

When Dallben saw that Taran was frightening the birds, he scolded him. "It's your job to look after Hen Wen," he said, "and it's time for her bath."

"Bah!" muttered Taran, as Hen Wen splashed happily in her tub. "A brave warrior like me should not be pampering pigs."

Just then, Hen Wen jumped up and stared around her with a look of terror on her face.

"What's wrong, Hen?" asked Taran. Concerned, he picked up the quivering pig to calm her.

"Bring her inside," said Dallben, adding to himself, "I was right, then."

In the cottage, Dallben filled a basin of water and lit a candle. "Tell no one what you are about to see," he warned Taran.

Then Dallben stirred the water and recited a magic spell. Hen Wen stared into the swirling water as Taran watched in wonder.

Suddenly, the surface of the water began to glow like molten gold. Then a terrifying vision appeared – a great cauldron overshadowed by a hideous horned shape.

"It's the Horned King!" cried Dallben. "He is coming back to destroy us!"

Hen Wen, in a trance, continued to stare into the basin. As the vision faded, her image appeared in the water.

More frightened than ever, Dallben explained to Taran: "The Horned King is searching for the Black Cauldron, which will restore him to power. Now he has discovered the secret of Hen Wen's visions. You must hide her in the forest until I come for you. If the Horned King captures Hen Wen and uses her power to find the Black Cauldron, he will destroy us all!"

Hurriedly, Dallben packed some bread in a bag and waved good-bye to Taran and Hen Wen.

"I won't fail you," promised Taran. Then he and Hen Wen set off into the forest.

The two companions stopped to drink when they came to a stream. As Taran bent over the swirling water, he saw a vision of a knight in full armor.

"Who is that?" gasped Taran. Beneath the gleaming helmet, he saw his own face.

"I shall be a warrior instead of a pigkeeper!" shouted Taran excitedly. "It was you who showed it to me, Hen Wen."

But when Taran turned around, Hen Wen was gone.

"Hen!" cried Taran in alarm. "Where are you? Come back!" The boy dashed into the forest, his heart hammering. He couldn't believe that he had failed in his mission to keep Hen Wen safe.

"Hen Wen!" he cried, cupping his hands around his mouth. "Come back!"

Hearing a noise in a nearby bush, Taran pulled an apple from his pocket. "Is that you, Hen Wen?" he called, moving toward the bush. "Come see the nice apple I've got for you."

Just then, a heavy weight landed on his shoulders and knocked him down! *"Ya-a-a-a!"* yelled his attacker, leaping after the apple as it rolled away. Imagine Taran's astonishment when he saw who had assaulted him − a small, furry creature with wild white hair and a bushy moustache. He was holding the apple behind his back.

"Oh, great prince, give poor starving Gurgi munchings and crunchings...nice apple," said the creature, looking hopefully at Taran. Then he turned toward the bushes with his prize.

"Oh, no, you don't!" cried Taran. "That's my apple!" But before he could get the apple away from Gurgi, Taran heard a shrill squealing sound. "It's Hen Wen!" he cried excitedly. "She's in trouble!"

A moment later, the little pig raced through the clearing at top speed. Right behind her was a huge winged gwythaint – a kind of flying dragon – about to seize her in its terrible claws!

"Must hide!" cried Gurgi in alarm. "Gwythaint come from Horned King's castle...very bad place." He dove into the bushes, but Taran ran to Hen Wen's rescue – just as the gwythaint caught her in its claws.

Desperately, Taran clutched the monster's tail, but it shook him off and rose into the air with the squealing Hen Wen. She was carried away to a dark, distant castle.

Taran tore after the gwythaint, but by the time he reached the gloomy castle, the winged shape had disappeared into a tower.

Taran took a flying leap at a vine that climbed the tower. Avoiding the vine's sharp thorns, he made his way up the steep wall. "I mustn't look down," he muttered to steady himself. But Gurgi's last words of warning still echoed in his ears: "Don't go! Don't go! No one comes back from Horned King's castle!"

At last, trembling from the strain, Taran reached a lighted window. With one last push, he heaved himself over the sill and stared about him.

Far below was a great crowd of rough-looking warriors – the Horned King's henchmen. Gathered around a crude table, they roared with cruel laughter and chanted bloodcurdling threats against their enemies. Taran stood frozen with fear.

Luckily for Taran, the warriors were so busy waving their swords and horn cups that they didn't notice him perched high above them.

"Prydain will soon be ours!" shouted one henchman.

Then a green dwarf hopped onto a barrel and speared a piece of meat on the table.

"Get out, Creeper!" yelled another henchman, lunging at the dwarf.

Suddenly, an icy wind stirred the wall hangings; the candles flickered and went out. Everyone fell silent in fear, and a loud explosion filled the hall with smoke. Taran saw a dark shape crowned with horns standing in an archway.

Henchmen, gwythaints, even the dogs drew back as the menacing figure moved toward the throne at one end of the hall.

"Welcome, Your Majesty," said the dwarf, busily dusting the steps to the throne.

"Silence!" boomed a deep, hollow voice. "Where is the prisoner? The pig must be made to reveal the hiding place of the Black Cauldron!"

"At once, Your Majesty!" cried the dwarf, racing away to the dungeon.

"I must hurry!" whispered Taran, plunging into a dark tunnel. He ran down a flight of stairs until he saw a light coming from Hen Wen's cell.

The dwarf threatened Hen Wen with a hot coal. "I warn you..." he said cruelly – just as Taran burst into the dungeon.

"Don't!" cried the boy.

Smirking, Creeper dragged Taran and Hen Wen back to the great hall. There, the Horned King beckoned them toward the throne.

"I presume you are the keeper of this pig?" demanded the King.

"Um, uh, y-y-yes, Sir," replied Taran, trembling.

"Then instruct her to show me the whereabouts of the Black Cauldron!"

A barrel of water was placed at the foot of the steps. Taran murmured to Hen Wen, "I'm sorry, Hen. You've got to show him...I can't let him kill you."

Taran recited the words of the magic spell, and Hen Wen began to go into a trance. A faint image of the Black Cauldron appeared in the water.

"Yes!" screamed the Horned King, leaping from his throne.

Taran was so startled that he jumped up and tipped over the barrel of water! Seizing Hen Wen in his arms, he raced from the hall.

"After them!" cried the dwarf, and the henchmen ran down the corridor in pursuit.

"It's okay, Hen" whispered Taran, holding tightly to the frightened pig. "We'll get away."

Behind them, Creeper was still yelling, "Catch them! After them!"

Taran dashed through an open door and bolted it behind him.
Only then did he see that they had reached a dead end – on a
balcony high over the moat. Creeper and the henchmen broke
down the door as Taran struggled to lift Hen Wen over the parapet.

"Swim, Hen!" the boy cried, letting her go just as Creeper
grabbed his foot. The henchmen seized him and dragged him off
to the dungeon.

Taran sat in the cobwebbed
dungeon, brooding about his
problem, until something caught
his attention. A bright ball of light
floated up into his gloomy prison
from a hole in the floor. A
beautiful girl climbed out after it.

"I'm Princess Eilonwy," said
the girl. "Another prisoner of the
Horned King. He thought my
magic bauble could lead him to
some old cauldron."

"That's why he took my pig,"
said Taran.

"I was hoping you were a warrior who could help me escape," said Eilonwy, disappointed.

"No," said Taran dejectedly. "I'm just an assistant pigkeeper who *wanted* to be a warrior."

"Well, come with me if you like," said the Princess, stepping back into the hole. Taran followed her and found himself standing on some beams above the ground. He jumped down, and the sparkling bauble led them through a dark corridor. Rats scurried past them, running from the bauble's light.

43

They followed the light of the bauble through underground passageways and ghostly caves. Eventually, they came to an eerie cavern where the air was ice-cold. "A burial chamber," said Eilonwy, shivering.

Before them stood a high stone tomb, where the carved image of a fallen king rested. Cautiously, Taran approached the cobwebbed figure and saw something glinting in the darkness. Breathless, he lifted a magnificent sword from the tomb.

Suddenly, a strange noise made him jump. "Is that a voice?" whispered Eilonwy.

Peering into another underground cell, Taran and Eilonwy were shocked to see a man tied up there. He was calling to one of the henchmen, "But you don't realize who I am! There's some mistake! I'm Fflewddur Fflam, minstrel of minstrels, balladeer to the grandest courts..."

The henchman paid no attention and passed by.

Taran and Eilonwy slipped into Fflewddur's cell. "Shhhh," cautioned Taran as he untied the minstrel. "We'll soon have you out of here."

The three companions stole
into the corridor, about to make
their escape, when they heard
cries of alarm and the clang of
weapons!

"They know we're missing!"
cried Eilonwy.

The henchmen were closing in
on them.

"Get behind me!" ordered
Taran. "I have the sword."

Just then, a brutal henchman wielding an axe emerged from the darkness and lunged at Taran. The boy raised the sword to fend off the blow, and the axe fell to pieces in a burst of light! "The sword is magic!" cried Taran.

Taran, Eilonwy, and Fflewddur ran down a passage and up a stair, with the henchmen close behind them. Through a door and around a corner, they found themselves at the drawbridge.

"Run!" cried Taran. He stopped and swung at the drawbridge chain with his magic sword. The chain broke and the gate fell, just as the three companions dashed under it.

At last Taran, Eilonwy, and Fflewddur stopped to rest. They had broken out of the Horned King's castle and escaped from the clutches of his henchmen. Now, they sat by a river in a forest glade, making plans. Taran told his companions about Hen Wen, while Eilonwy mended a rip in Fflewddur's pants and Fflewddur made up a song about their adventures.

Suddenly, they heard a rustling in the woods nearby. A furry
white head popped out of the tree's roots.

"It's Gurgi," said Taran with delight.

"Kind master, good master. Gurgi has found tracks of the piggy.
If Gurgi shows master the piggy's tracks, will kind master give
Gurgi munchings and crunchings?"

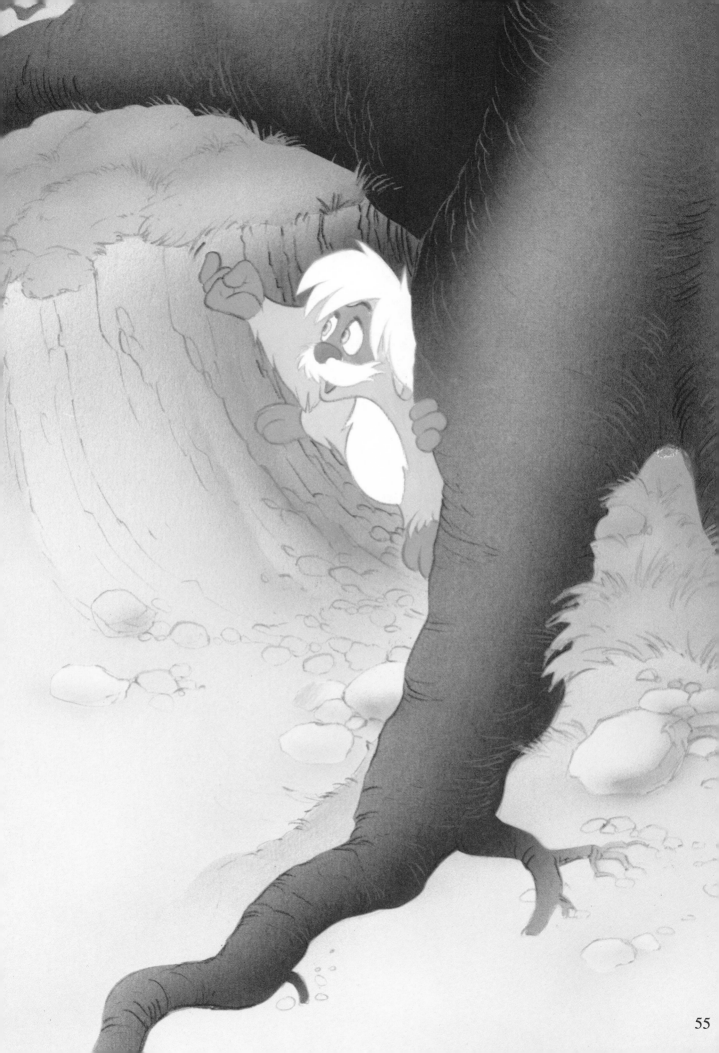

"You've found Hen Wen?" cried Taran. "Please, Gurgi, show us the way."

The little creature led the way into a cavern, where the tracks of a pig were clearly marked in the sand of the cave's floor.

By the light of Eilonwy's bauble, they followed the tracks to a deep lake in the heart of the cave.

"See?" said Gurgi. "The piggy has been here."

"But where did she go?" asked Taran, puzzled, for the tracks led straight to the edge of the lake.

Gurgi began to cross the water on stepping stones, but once he reached the lake's center, the water began to whirl around him. The whirlpool was sucking him under! Gurgi cried, "Help, master!"

"Hold on!" cried Taran, reaching for him. But Gurgi clutched him so tightly that Taran, too, was drawn into the whirlpool. When Eilonwy tried to save Taran, pulling Fflewddur behind her, all four of them sank beneath the water!

They found themselves in another cave, below the lake. Several Fair Folk circled overhead, then hurried to tell their king of the new arrivals.

King Eidilleg came to greet his visitors, and Taran found Hen Wen there among the Fair Folk, safe and sound. He also learned that the Black Cauldron was hidden in the land of Morva.

"My servant, Doli, will guide you there," said the king. Then he sprinkled the travellers with fairy dust and sent them on their way.

Moments later, Doli alighted on a tree stump in the middle of an evil-smelling marsh. "There it is," said Doli, pointing to a tumble-down cottage. "The hiding place of the Black Cauldron."

"Bless my soul," said Fflewddur, "what are all those frogs doing here?"

"Those aren't frogs, they're people," said Doli. He explained that the three witches who lived in the cottage had changed their victims into frogs. Then he wished them luck and started home.

"I not like this place," muttered Gurgi.

"Let's hope no one's home," said Taran, pushing open the creaky cottage door.

Inside the dark cottage, unseen eyes watched from a high shelf as the four companions searched for the Black Cauldron. Suddenly, there was a great explosion. A mountain of cauldrons appeared before them. In the smoke, they made out fearful forms of three witches: Orgoch, Orddu and Orwen.

"You evil people!" shrieked Orddu. "You shall all be turned into frogs...and eaten!"

"Nice to meet you, ladies,"
said Fflewddur. "Good-bye,
now!" But as he turned to flee,
Orwen grabbed his cape and
pulled him close to her.

"My, my," she said admiringly,
"aren't you handsome! And what
a lovely harp. Don't you find me
irresistible?"

Fflewddur stammered, "Yes!
Ah, well, of course...most
attractive." As he tried to back
away, Orwen's sister, Orgoch,
snapped, "Enough of this
lovesick nonsense!"

Orgoch pointed at Fflewddur and a sharp *Zap!* of electricity crackled through the room. Instantly, Fflewddur disappeared. In his place was a frog, trapped in the bodice of Orwen's dress.

"Great Beelin!" croaked Fflewddur.

"Enough!" shouted Taran, waving his sword. "We've come for the Black Cauldron! Give it to us!"

Startled, Orwen dropped the frog, and Fflewddur appeared, crouched on the floor. The three witches stared at Taran and his magic sword in amazement.

Then Orddu asked slyly, "What will you give us in exchange for the Cauldron?"

"I'll give my dearest possession," answered Taran. "My sword."

"No, Taran!" cried Eilonwy, but the boy paid no attention.

"Agreed!" said Orddu. "We have made a bargain." In a flash of light, the sword vanished from Taran's hand. Then the cottage itself disappeared.

The travellers found themselves lying face-down on the ground. An earthquake rumbled around them, and the Black Cauldron appeared, pushing up from beneath the ground.

Taran rose, picked up a broken tree limb and lunged at the Cauldron. The witches laughed mockingly from above.

"The Black Cauldron can never be destroyed!" called Orddu. "Only its evil powers can be stopped!"

"But how?" asked Taran.

The witches' answer chilled his blood. "Someone must climb into it of his own free will – never to return alive!"

With that, the witches vanished.

The little group looked around sadly, unsure of what to do. Then they felt the cold shadow of a gwythaint pass over them. Three henchmen with sharp spears sprang from behind a tree.

"Pig boy!" shouted one of the henchmen triumphantly.

Gurgi, hiding behind the tree, gasped fearfully, "Oh-oh...trouble...good-bye!" He ran for cover.

Taran, Eilonwy, and Fflewddur were taken back to the Horned King's castle, along with the Black Cauldron. The king gloated over his capture of the Cauldron and laughed mockingly at his prisoners. "Such a brave and handsome group – a pig boy, a scullery maid and a broken-down minstrel!"

"Oh, thank you very much," whispered Fflewddur indignantly.

But the evil king had already turned back to the Cauldron. Raising his hands high, he cried, "Army of the dead – arise!"

The three captives watched in horror as a phantom army rose from the Black Cauldron. Ghoulish skeletons, armed with axes and swords, marched through the smoke in ever-growing numbers. Creeper, the dwarf, cheered the advance of the terrible army, but even the henchmen fled before the Cauldron Born.

Taran, Eilonwy, and Fflewddur stared at one another hopelessly, as they saw the fate that awaited their land – and themselves.

"Oh, I wish I'd stayed a frog," said Fflewddur sadly. "I was so much happier..."

But Gurgi had not forgotten his friends.

"Psssst, master," he whispered from the arch above.

"Gurgi!" cried Taran, relieved. "What are you doing here?"

"Gurgi set you free; then we leave this evil place."

As soon as Gurgi freed him, Taran sprang from the arch to a ledge that overlooked the boiling Cauldron.

Suddenly, Eilonwy realized what Taran meant to do. "No! Don't!" she cried.

"No, master!" echoed Gurgi, running to block Taran. "Not go into evil Cauldron!"

"I must stop it!" cried Taran. But Gurgi was too quick for him. Shutting his eyes tightly, he leaped headlong into the Cauldron!

"*No!*" cried Taran, covering his face. "*Oh, no!*"

As Gurgi disappeared, an enormous explosion rocked the throne room. Outside, the drawbridge collapsed, throwing thousands of phantom warriors into the moat. All over the castle, the Cauldron Born disintegrated into heaps of bones.

Last of all, screaming his fury, the Horned King was sucked into the Black Cauldron. "My power cannot di-i-i-e-e!" he shrieked − and vanished from the earth.

"Run for your lives!" shouted Taran.

Fleeing through the dark corridors, the three companions saw the floors open up to swallow both henchmen and gwythaints as they tried to escape. Deep under the earth, at the castle's water gate, they found a small boat. They leaped aboard and Fflewddur poled them to safety, even as the Horned King's castle crumbled into ruin.

The travellers left the boat with heavy hearts, thinking of their brave friend, Gurgi. Looking back, they saw the Black Cauldron floating on the water; the witches appeared in the clouds above it.

"Now that the Cauldron's no use to you," said Orddu, "we'll just take it and be on our way."

"Not so fast," Fflewddur replied. "What do you offer in return?"

"The magic sword," said Orgoch.

"What does a pig boy need with a sword?" asked Taran. "I have another offer: the Cauldron for Gurgi."

"We have made a bargain!" laughed Orddu.

The Cauldron began to spin wildly in the water. Then it rose from the surface in a whirlwind of white light and touched down briefly on the shore. When it whirled away, the still form of Gurgi lay before them.

Tearfully, the group ran to Gurgi's side and knelt down. Taran lifted Gurgi tenderly and hugged him. Fflewddur was silent, but Eilonwy began to sob.

Suddenly, Taran felt a small paw slipping into his vest, as if in search of an apple.

"Gurgi," he stammered in disbelief, "you're alive!"

Gurgi felt himself carefully to make sure he was really alive.

"Great Beelin!" shouted Fflewddur. "He's alive!"

"Oh, Fflewddur!" cried Eilonwy, jumping for joy.

"I'm alive!" said Gurgi happily, clinging to Taran. "Look! Touch me!"

Eilonwy drew closer to give him a kiss and ended up kissing Taran as well.

Blushing, Taran said, "Come on, let's go home!"

"Gurgi's happy day!" agreed Gurgi.

Hand in hand, the friends set out on the long journey home.

Meanwhile, at Dallben's farm, Hen Wen watched them in a pool of water. The Fair Folk had brough her home once she was out of danger.

Together Hen Wen and Dallben awaited the return of the heroes. And all of Prydain rejoiced that the evil power of the Horned King and the Black Cauldron had been banished from the land.